★ THE ADVENTURES OF ★
TINTIN

The Chapter Book

Adapted by Stephanie Peters

Based on the screenplay by
Steven Moffat and
Edgar Wright & Joe Cornish

Based on The Adventures of Tintin
series by Hergé

BANTAM BOOKS

THE ADVENTURES OF TINTIN: THE CHAPTER BOOK
A BANTAM BOOK 978 0 857 51075 4

First published in the United States in 2011 by Little Brown

First published in Great Britain by Bantam,
an imprint of Random House Children's Books
A Random House Group Company

Bantam edition published 2011

1 3 5 7 9 10 8 6 4 2

Bantam Books are published by Random House Children's Books,
61–63 Uxbridge Road, London W5 5SA

www.**kids**at**randomhouse**.co.uk
www.**totallyrandombooks**.co.uk
www.**randomhouse**.co.uk

Addresses for companies within The Random House Group Limited can be found
at: www.randomhouse.co.uk/offices.htm

THE RANDOM HOUSE GROUP Limited Reg. No. 954009

A CIP catalogue record for this book is available from the British Library.

Printed in Great Britain by Print 4 Limited.

★ THE ADVENTURES OF ★
TINTIN

★ THE ADVENTURES OF ★
TINTIN

★

CHAPTER ONE

The *Unicorn*

Tintin was a young reporter with a nose for news. He and his trusty white terrier, Snowy, were always stumbling upon good stories and wild adventures. But lately—

"There's nothing going on!" Tintin complained to Snowy. "I can't call myself a reporter if there isn't any news!"

Snowy gave a sad *woof*.

Tintin and Snowy were walking through the local marketplace that sold all sorts of odds and ends. As they passed one booth, Tintin spotted a model of an old-fashioned sailing ship. His eyes lit up. "Triple-masted, double decks, fifty guns—isn't she a beauty, Snowy? I'm going to buy her!"

He paid the vendor and took the ship. "She's called the *Unicorn*," he said, reading the nameplate as he held the model high to admire it.

"The *Unicorn*?" A tall man with a coal-black beard pushed through the crowd. "I'll give you double what you paid for her, Mister...?"

"The name's Tintin. Who are you? And why do you want my model?"

"I am Ivan Ivanovitch Sakharine," the man replied. "This model once belonged to the late sea captain Sir Francis Haddock. Haddock lost his fortune

when his ship, the real *Unicorn*, sank." He touched the *Unicorn*'s mast and smiled. "My family and the Haddocks go way back. I wish to return the model to their estate, Marlinspike Hall. So name your price!"

Just then, Snowy growled. Tintin glanced down. His dog was staring at Sakharine with his teeth bared and ears flat.

Snowy doesn't trust him, Tintin thought. *And if Snowy doesn't trust him, then neither do I!*

He tucked the model firmly under his arm. "I'm sorry, but the *Unicorn* isn't for sale."

Sakharine's smile vanished. "That is…unfortunate, Mr Tintin." He spun on his heel and swept away with a flourish.

Snowy started after him, but Tintin called him back. "It's okay, boy," he said. "He's gone." Yet as they headed for home, Tintin couldn't shake the feeling that Sakharine was watching their every move.

Back at their apartment, at 26 Labrador Street, Tintin put the ship on a table and opened a window. But more than fresh air came in!

"Hey!" Tintin yelled as a scruffy white cat leaped into the kitchen.

Barking excitedly, Snowy gave chase across the couch, under a chair, onto the table holding the model, and –

"Great snakes! Look out!" cried Tintin.

Snowy skidded right into the ship. *Crash!* The *Unicorn* hit the floor, its mast snapping in two.

"Bad dog!" Tintin scolded. He picked up the broken model, and a small metal tube rolled out of the mast.

"What the –?" Curious, Tintin opened the tube. Inside was a very old piece of parchment covered in spidery handwriting.

"*Three Unicorns in company sailing in the noonday sun will speak,*" Tintin read. "*For 'tis from the light that light will dawn.*"

Beneath the words were some strange symbols.

Tintin stared at the parchment in wonder. "What can it mean?"

CHAPTER TWO

★

Robbed!

Try as he might, Tintin couldn't figure out the riddle. At last, he put the parchment in his wallet, put his wallet in his pocket, and whistled to Snowy. "Let's go to the library to learn more about the *Unicorn*."

With his terrier trotting beside him, Tintin hurried outside—and right into two men in black suits and bowler hats.

"Thompson—and Thomson!"

"Tintin!" The men were almost identical. Only their mustaches gave them away. They worked for the International Criminal Police Organization, better known as Interpol.

"Are you on assignment?" Tintin asked.

"No," Thompson replied. "We're on a sidewalk."

"We're also on a job," Thomson added. "A light-fingered fiend has the city in his grip!"

"A pickpocket?" Tintin said.

The policemen nodded. "No wallet –" Thompson warned.

"Or purse –" Thomson put in.

"Is safe!" they finished together.

"Picking a pocket is childishly simple," Thompson said.

"Or simply childish," Thomson offered. "Best be on your guard!"

Tintin promised to be careful and continued on to the library. There, he found a book about the *Unicorn*. He settled into a chair and began to read.

"*Sir Francis Haddock set sail in 1676. His ship, the* Unicorn, *was rumored to carry a fabulous treasure. If so, that treasure was lost at sea when the* Unicorn *was attacked by pirates. The ship sank and all hands were lost. Only Sir Francis survived. He never spoke of the tragedy, but spent his remaining days crafting three models of his doomed vessel.*"

"So there are three models," Tintin muttered. "I wonder where the other two are."

He read the entry's last sentence: "*Legend has it that these models hold secrets that lead to the long-lost treasure.*"

Tintin closed the book. "I bet that Sakharine fellow knows about the treasure. That's why he wanted my ship so badly!" He stood up. "Come on, Snowy. I want to keep an eye on our *Unicorn*!"

They left the library and headed for home. Suddenly—*wham!*—an old man appeared out of nowhere and crashed headlong into Tintin!

"Oh, I beg your pardon!" the old man apologized, brushing dirt from Tintin's coat.

"No harm done," Tintin reassured him. Then he bid the man good day, hurried up to his apartment, opened the door – and froze.

His place had been ransacked. The *Unicorn* was gone!

Tintin shook his head angrily. "At least I still have the scroll." He reached for his wallet. But to his horror, his coat pocket was empty!

"I've been robbed – twice!"

He snapped his fingers. "That old man – I bet he's the pickpocket! We've got to find him!"

He ran down the stairs, but his way was blocked by two burly men carrying a large crate.

"Mr. Tintin? Delivery for ya."

"I didn't order anything!"

"That's because you're the delivery!"

Strong arms grabbed him from behind, and a hand pressed a handkerchief to his face. Tintin's eyes widened.

He was being kidnapped!

CHAPTER THREE

The *Karaboudjan*

Tintin groaned. "Where am I?" He tried to sit up, but his hands and feet were tied.

"You're on board the *Karaboudjan*." A figure loomed out of the shadows.

"Sakharine!"

"The same." Sakharine tapped a silver-tipped cane against the palm of his hand. "Now, where is it?"

"Where's what?" Tintin replied innocently.

Sakharine produced a slip of parchment identical to the one Tintin had found in the model ship. "Where is the scroll from your *Unicorn*?"

"Does it look just like that?" Tintin asked.

"Yes."

"And it has a poem written on it?"

"Yes!"

"It was hidden in the mast?"

"*Yes!*" the villain shouted.

"I don't have it," Tintin replied calmly.

Sakharine's face darkened with fury. With one swift movement, he unsheathed a sword hidden in his cane and shook it at Tintin. "Don't lie to me!"

"It's not on him, boss." The kidnapping thugs stepped into the room. "We searched him."

"Yeah, we searched him," the other one echoed.

Sakharine swung around and pointed the sword at his henchmen. "Fools! I wanted that scroll, not this... *boy*! Without it, the other two *Unicorn* parchments are useless!"

Tintin wanted to ask Sakharine if he knew where the third scroll was. Then he eyed the sword and decided that Sakharine wasn't going to tell him.

A shout came from the deck above. "The captain is awake!"

"Bah! Must I see to everything myself?" Sakharine swept out of the room with the thugs at his heels. Just before the door slammed shut, a white blur darted into the room.

"Snowy!" Tintin whispered with joy. "How'd you find me?"

Snowy snuffed the floor. Then he lifted his head and sniffed the air.

"Clever dog! You followed your nose."

Snowy gave a short happy bark.

"Shhh!" Tintin warned. "Sakharine is still outside the door! Listen!"

They could hear the bad guys talking in the hallway outside. "After you deal with the captain," Sakharine said, "find out where that boy has put the scroll!"

"Righto!" one of the thugs said. "Er, and then what?"

"Throw him overboard!" Sakharine snapped. "And then jump in after him."

Tintin gulped. "Snowy, chew through these ropes!" he whispered.

Snowy went to work, and in no time, Tintin was free. "Now to get us out of here!"

He took the rope to the room's one porthole, hoping to climb down and swim to shore. But that

plan was useless—he saw only water outside the window. "Nothing but ocean for miles!"

Then he looked up. Directly above was another porthole. He pulled his head back in and searched the room. He found two short planks of wood in a corner.

Moving quickly and quietly, he tied the planks together with the rope. Then, holding one end of the rope, he leaned out the porthole and tossed the boards toward the opening above as if he were throwing a lasso. The planks sailed through the porthole above on the second throw, caught against the inside, and held fast.

"Hop on, Snowy!"

Hand over hand, Tintin hauled them up. They squeezed through the small window and fell onto the floor.

"We did it, boy! We're safe!"

Safe, yes – but not alone!

"Blistering barnacles!" a deep voice boomed. "Who are you?"

★

CHAPTER FOUR

Captain Haddock

Tintin jumped back. Scowling at him from across the room was a weather-beaten sailor with a thick black beard and bushy eyebrows.

"I'm Tintin. Who are you?" he asked the sailor.

"I am the captain of this ship!" the man answered. "Or I was, until my first mate double-crossed me. I've been locked in here for days!"

"Locked in?" Tintin tried the door handle. It turned easily.

The captain blinked. "It's not locked?"

"Not." Tintin opened the door – and came face-to-face with one of the thugs!

"I found him!" the man cried gleefully. "I –"

The captain took a swing and the henchman crumpled to the floor.

"Thank you," Tintin said.

"Pleasure," the captain replied. "Tintin, did you say your name was?"

Tintin nodded. "And you're...?"

"Captain Archibald Haddock."

Tintin's jaw dropped. "Haddock? Any relation to Sir Francis Haddock?"

"He was my great-great-great-great-great–er, how many *great*s was that? No matter. He was my ancestor."

Tintin started pacing. "I bet Sakharine stole your ship because he thinks you have inside information about the treasure. Tell me, do you know the *real* story of the wreck of the *Unicorn*?"

Haddock drew himself up to his full height. "Of course! The secret of that ship has been passed down from Haddock to Haddock for generations. My granddaddy himself told it to me from his deathbed."

"What did he tell you?" Tintin asked eagerly.

"I – I don't remember," the captain confessed. "My memory isn't what it used to be."

"What did it used to be?"

"I've forgotten," Haddock said.

Just then, Snowy growled a warning. The thug was stirring. Tintin tried to lift him. "Help me with him, will you?"

Haddock nodded and punched the thug again. The man slumped like a rag doll.

"I meant, help me drag him into the room," Tintin said.

"Oh." Together, they locked the unconscious man in the cabin.

"Now to get off this ship," Tintin said. "Any suggestions?"

"A lifeboat," Haddock replied. "Follow me!"

They tiptoed up the stairs and into a dark hallway. Suddenly, Tintin stopped, put a finger to his lips, and pointed to a door marked *Radio Room*. Strange clicks and sounds were coming from inside.

"Morse code," Tintin whispered.

The sounds stopped. "Here's the message you've been waiting for, sir," someone inside the room said.

"Read it!"

Tintin and Haddock exchanged startled looks. Sakharine!

"*The Milanese Nightingale has landed in Bagghar,*" the radioman read.

Sakharine gave a low laugh. "Excellent! My secret weapon is in place. Soon the third scroll will be mine!"

A shadow darkened the floor under the radio room door. The door handle started to turn.

"He's coming out!" Tintin hissed. "Hide!"

CHAPTER FIVE

⭐

Sea, Air, and Sand

Tintin, Haddock, and Snowy ducked into a nearby room. Tintin peeked through a crack and watched Sakharine and the radioman hurry off.

"Take Snowy to the lifeboat. I'm going to dig up some more information," Tintin told Haddock. The reporter in him smelled more to the story.

Haddock and Snowy disappeared up the stairs. Tintin slipped into the radio room. He saw on the desk a brochure labeled *The Port of Bagghar*. He glanced at it and gasped. The front cover featured a photo of another *Unicorn* model ship!

He pocketed the brochure, then sat down and tapped out a short message. That done, he sneaked up to the deck to find Haddock and Snowy.

Crack! A shot rang out and a bullet whizzed past his ear!

"Tintin! Over here!" Haddock waved frantically from a lifeboat.

Haddock lowered the boat as Tintin vaulted over the railing and into the craft.

"Row!" Tintin cried, grabbing an oar.

"As if our lives depended upon it?"

"Yes!" Tintin shouted as another bullet zipped past him. "Because they do!"

Tintin and Haddock pulled hard at the oars. The huge *Karaboudjan*, struggling to turn around, fell behind.

"Those mutant malingerers will never catch us!" Haddock said triumphantly.

Just then, a seaplane appeared above.

"Then again . . ." Tintin said.

Rat-a-tat-tat! Gunfire peppered the water around them!

Tintin found a signal flare in the lifeboat and

aimed it at the plane. *Twang!* The flare went right into the plane's engine, and black smoke started to billow out.

"You got 'em!" Haddock cheered. "You – uh-oh!"

The damaged plane was spiraling straight for them!

"Great snakes! Jump!"

They leaped overboard. The lifeboat capsized. The seaplane hit the water and bobbed up on its pontoons.

Tintin, Snowy, and the captain surfaced behind their boat. They watched as the pilots climbed out of the cockpit to stand on the pontoons and repair the damage.

"Stay here." Tintin slipped beneath the waves and swam underwater. Moments later, he emerged beside the plane.

"Almost fixed," one pilot said. He twisted some wires together. "There!"

That's what Tintin had been waiting for. "Put your hands in the air!" he cried from behind them. The frightened pilots assumed the worst and put their arms over their heads.

Five minutes later – manual in one hand, controls in the other – Tintin was flying the seaplane with Haddock in the co-pilot seat. Snowy was curled up comfortably in Tintin's lap. The pilots had been left in the lifeboat, bobbing along in the waves.

Tintin scanned the water down below. "Look! The *Karaboudjan*!"

Haddock grinned, thinking of their brilliant escape. But when he looked up, his happiness was replaced by terror.

"Tintin! Look out for that wall of death!" There was a vast storm cloud in front of them.

Too late! The plane flew right into the raging storm! The blue sky was replaced with black swirling clouds. Rain pelted the windows. Thunder shook the hull. Bolts of lightning flashed all around them.

"Hold on!" Tintin pointed the plane's nose down. The plane dropped out of the storm – and straight towards massive sand dunes!

Now Tintin pulled back on the controls, fighting

to bring the nose back up. But it was no use.

Boom! The plane hit the ground, flipped end over end, and then skidded to a halt deep in a mountain of sand.

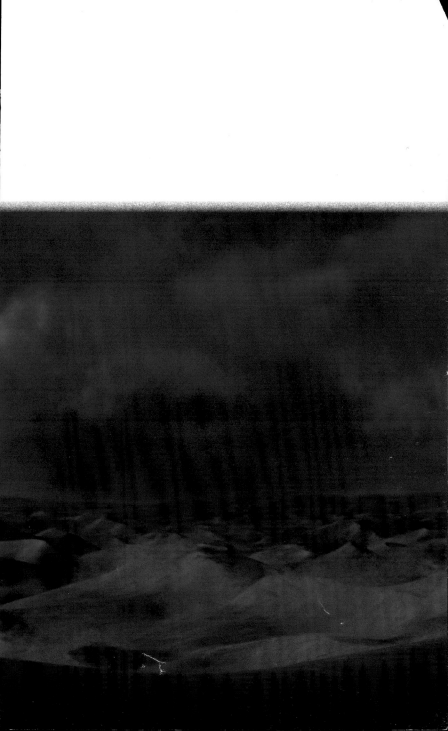

★

CHAPTER SIX

The Memory Remembered

"Ooooh!" Tintin groaned. "Now I know how a scrambled egg feels!"

Snowy bounded up through the sand. Tintin patted his furry best friend, and then he spotted Haddock standing at the top of a dune.

"What beach is this?" the captain asked when Tintin joined him.

"It's not a beach. It's the Sahara desert."

Haddock fell to his knees. "The land of thirst! We're doomed! We're—wait! What's that?"

He staggered up, staring at something in the distance. "Water! We're saved!" He tumbled down the dune.

"It's just a mirage!" Tintin cried in alarm. "You're seeing things that aren't there!"

He was right. When he caught up with Haddock, the captain was hallucinating. But he wasn't seeing water.

"Did you ever see a more beautiful sight?" Haddock said dreamily. "Triple-masted, double decks, fifty guns…"

Tintin gasped. "You see…the *Unicorn*?"

"Aye," Haddock said. "And I'm her captain, Sir Francis Haddock!"

Tintin's mind whirled. *Haddock's memory of his family is coming back!*

"What else do you see?" he asked softly.

Haddock's face darkened. "Another ship! And she's flying the Jolly Roger!"

"The *Unicorn* is being attacked by pirates?"

"Aye!" Captain Haddock brandished an imaginary sword. "They're boarding! It's a fight to the death! No prisoners taken—and no mercy given!"

He slashed and parried against unseen foes. But Sir Francis and his men must have lost the fight, for the captain suddenly dropped his arms as he continued to act out his ancestor's story.

"He's taken my ship," he whispered.

"Who?" Tintin pressed.

"A pirate whose very name strikes terror in the hearts of men," the captain said, his voice still hushed. "Red Rackham! He knows the *Unicorn* has treasure hidden in her hold. He's forced my men to walk the plank and now threatens me with death. But he didn't count on one thing."

The captain threw back his shoulders. "I'm a Haddock, and a Haddock always has a trick up his sleeve. I'll sink my *Unicorn* before I let him have her!"

Haddock sprinkled a handful of sand in a line. "A gunpowder fuse that leads to the ammunitions room should do the trick."

He pantomimed touching a lit match to the gunpowder. "Revenge is mine!" he cried, moving away from the imaginary flame. "The *Unicorn* and her treasure will never be yours!"

With a triumphant yell, Haddock leaped from the top of the dune to the sand below. "The mighty explosion rocks the sea!"

He whipped off his hat and held it like a bowl. "Treasure rains from the sky! Some lands in my hat, but most sinks into the watery depths to join the *Unicorn*, the pirates...and my men."

His last words came out as only a whisper. Then suddenly, he shuddered.

"But it's not over yet! With his last breath, Red Rackham curses me and my family!"

Haddock's voice changed. Tintin realized he was hearing Rackham's final words.

"We will meet again, Haddock! In another time! In another life!"

With that, Haddock collapsed in the sand and was still.

★

CHAPTER SEVEN

Sakharine's Secret Weapon

"Captain! Are you okay?"

Haddock blinked several times. "Great blistering barnacles! How could I have been so blind?"

"Why? What is it?"

"Not what—*who*! Before my granddaddy died, he showed me a painting of Red Rackham. He looked just like Sakharine!"

"Sakharine is descended from Rackham?"

Haddock turned pale. "Sakharine is after the treasure—*and* my life! He wants vengeance for his ancestor's death."

"Well, he won't succeed," Tintin said. "We'll stop him!"

"How? We don't know where he or the scrolls are!"

"Oh yes we do!" Tintin pulled out the Bagghar brochure and showed Haddock the photo of the *Unicorn*. "If I'm right, he's after this. So…to Bagghar?"

Haddock stood up. "To Bagghar!" Then he paused. "It could be a long walk, you know."

As if on cue, Snowy appeared at the top of a dune leading two camels with their reins held in his teeth.

"I don't know how you do it, boy," Tintin said as he climbed onto his humpbacked mount, "but I sure am glad you do!"

Thanks to the camels, Tintin, Snowy, and Haddock reached Bagghar in no time.

"The brochure says the *Unicorn* is kept in the palace." Tintin pointed to an ornate building looming on the horizon. "There it is!"

They hadn't gone far when they ran into a huge throng of cheering people.

"Make way for the world-famous opera singer, the Milanese Nightingale!"

The crowd parted to let a solidly built woman dripping with jewels pass.

Tintin and Haddock stared at her and then at each other. "*That's* Sakharine's secret weapon?"

"What kind of weapon is an opera singer?" Haddock wondered.

Tintin spied a poster advertising the diva's concert. It was scheduled for that afternoon at the palace. "It's perfect!" he told Haddock. "We can keep an eye on the Nightingale and find the *Unicorn* at the same time."

An hour later, they walked into the palace theater. Tintin saw the *Unicorn* immediately. It was housed in a bulletproof glass case right near the stage. He started toward it, only to be stopped by two heavily armed guards.

"No one goes near the ship," one growled.

At least Sakharine can't get near it, either, Tintin thought as he returned to his seat.

Then the hall lights dimmed and the orchestra began to play. The Milanese Nightingale strode onto the stage, took a monstrously deep breath, and belted out a single note.

"LAAAAAAAAHHHHHHH!"

Her voice started down low but then rose slowly up the scale.

Haddock clutched his head. "*Aaahhh* is right! My ears are bleeding!"

A movement in the balcony caught Tintin's eye. He glanced up.

"Captain, look!"

"It's Sakharine!"

As the diva's voice trilled to a piercingly high note, Sakharine leaned forward eagerly. But he wasn't watching the singer. Instead, his fierce black eyes were glued to the *Unicorn*.

That's when Tintin figured out his secret weapon. He leaped to his feet. "Stop singing! That note is so high, it'll break—"

Crash! The sound of shattering glass drowned out his words. The *Unicorn's* case burst into a thousand pieces!

⭐

CHAPTER EIGHT

Three *Unicorns* Together

The theater erupted in chaos. Then high above the noise came a loud whistle. Tintin craned his neck and saw a falcon fly from the balcony. It swooped to the shattered case, snapped off the *Unicorn*'s mast, and flapped back up to land on Sakharine's arm!

With a crow of triumph, Sakharine swept away from the hallway.

Tintin and Haddock pushed through the crowd after him. They had just reached the hall when someone grabbed Tintin from behind!

Tintin whirled around to find two men wearing bowler hats standing there.

"Thompson – and Thomson!" Tintin cried in

disbelief. "What are you doing here?"

"We got your Morse code message describing the pickpocket," Thomson said.

Thompson nodded. "That pocket picker has picked his last pocket." He handed something to Tintin.

"Great snakes! My wallet!" He opened it and pulled out a piece of parchment. "The scroll! I've got it!"

"Correction: *I've* got it!"

Sakharine leaped out from behind a pillar and sent his falcon diving at Tintin's head.

Tintin threw up his hands to shield his face. The paper fluttered from his grasp. Sakharine snatched it in midair and raced away.

"After him!" Tintin cried.

Tintin, Snowy, and Haddock chased Sakharine through the halls, out onto the grounds, and into a vast garage filled with vehicles. There, Sakharine eluded them in the shadows until—*vroom!*—he sped past them in a jeep, his falcon flapping and shrieking on the windshield.

Tintin jumped onto a nearby motorcycle and kick-started the engine. "Come on!" he yelled to the others.

A palace guard appeared out of nowhere and aimed a rocket launcher right at Tintin. "Halt, thief!"

"Rowf!" A furry ball of white fury grabbed hold of the guard's ankle! He howled in pain and dropped his weapon as Snowy attacked.

Haddock seized the rocket launcher and jumped into the motorcycle's sidecar. Snowy bounded in after him and Tintin took off. They zigzagged through the streets of Bagghar, searching for Sakharine. They had just reached the harbor when –

"There he is!"

Sakharine's jeep darted out from a side street directly in front of them.

"This'll stop him!" Haddock roared. He aimed the rocket launcher at the jeep's wheels and fired. But instead of shooting forward, the rocket zoomed backward and hit a dam!

Boom! The dam exploded into a wall of water.

"Oops." Haddock looked behind them. "Er, you might want to step on it."

Tintin glanced in the rearview mirror. Water flowed through the town, filling once dry canals and gushing out of fountains. Townspeople surged into the streets to fill jugs with precious water. Tintin gunned the motor and roared up beside the jeep.

"Snowy, get the scrolls!"

But before Snowy could pounce, Sakharine thrust the parchments into his falcon's beak.

"Return to the *Karaboudjan*!" he ordered.

The falcon soared into the air. Suddenly, a beam of sunlight shone through the scrolls. Tintin stared. So did Sakharine. And in that instant, they both discovered the secret of the *Unicorn* scrolls.

"Captain! I have the answer! I – Captain?"

But Haddock was no longer in the sidecar. He was dangling from the cannon barrel of a huge tank!

"Tintin! Help!"

Three Brothers joyned.

company sailing in

will sp

For 'tis from the Ligh

down. And there

42 A

the Eagl

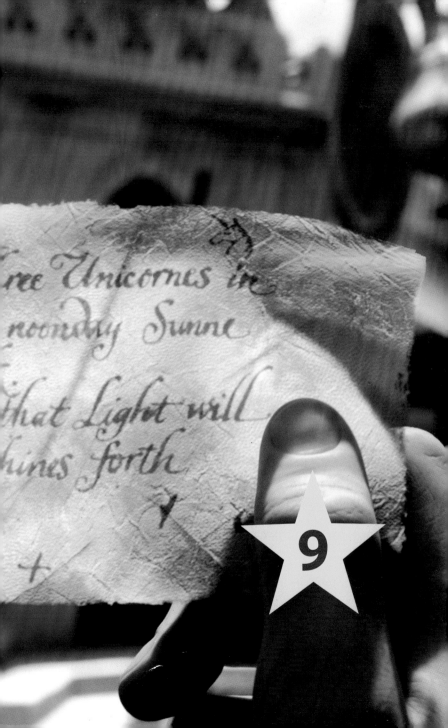

⭐

CHAPTER NINE

To Catch a Thief

Tintin gasped. The tank had snagged Haddock by the coat as it passed. Now it threatened to carry him over the edge of the road and into the sea!

Sakharine gave a gleeful shout and sped away. Tintin itched to go after him, but he couldn't abandon his friend. He veered next to the tank, edging the sidecar as close as he dared. Haddock struggled to free himself from his coat. Finally, he got loose and dropped back into his seat. And not a moment too soon, for the tank careened off the wall and sank like a stone.

"My favorite coat, gone," Haddock said sadly.

Tintin barely heard him. He was too busy watching

a ship sail out of the harbor.

"The *Karaboudjan*," he muttered as he stopped the bike. "It's gone, and the scrolls with it. We…failed."

Haddock climbed out of the sidecar. "Failed? Nonsense! There's something you need to know about failure, Tintin."

"Yes?"

"You can't let it defeat you. Besides, the solution is right under our noses! Look!" Haddock pointed.

Tintin turned. There, coasting in a bathtub through the mud, were Thompson and Thomson.

"Hello, Tintin!" they said when the tub came to a halt. "Can we give you a lift?"

"In that?"

"No, in our aircraft!"

Ten minutes later, Tintin, Haddock, Snowy, and the two policemen were flying in an Interpol seaplane far above the *Karaboudjan*.

Tintin gazed out the window. Suddenly, he sat forward. "Snowy, isn't that Labrador Street?" Snowy gave a happy woof when he saw his home.

"Why would Sakharine come back here?" Tintin didn't have an answer.

The sun was high in the sky when the plane set down not far from the *Karaboudjan*. While Thomson and Thompson stayed behind with the plane, Tintin, Haddock, and Snowy crept onto the dock and toward the ship. Halfway there, Tintin stopped. Before him was a large crane with its arm hovering directly over the *Karaboudjan*.

"There's our way on board," Tintin whispered. "I'll go first."

He climbed over the cab of the crane, shimmied up the metal arm, and then lowered himself down a chain to the deck below. He was about to let the others know he was safe when he heard the captain cry out in alarm. Tintin looked down – and froze.

Sakharine, his sword in one hand and the scrolls in the other, was advancing toward Haddock.

"You've lost, Haddock," Sakharine sneered. "Soon, the *Unicorn*'s treasure will be mine. But first, I'll take your *life*!" He suddenly lunged forward, the point of his sword aimed right at Haddock's heart!

Haddock dodged the thrust. Sakharine rushed past him, right to the edge of the dock!

Tintin held his breath, sure that Sakharine would fall, taking the scrolls with him. But Sakharine caught himself in time and whipped around to attack Haddock again.

That's when Tintin made his move. He swung out on the chain and snatched the scrolls from Sakharine's hand!

Sakharine howled in outrage. But his cry stopped short when Haddock's fist connected with his face. Sakharine staggered off the dock and was swallowed up by the water!

Haddock turned to Tintin. "Now let's see those scrolls."

Tintin handed him the parchments, one on top of the other. "*Three Unicorns in company sailing in the noonday sun will speak,*" he read.

"*For 'tis from the light that light will dawn,*" Haddock finished. He held up the scrolls. The sun shone through them, revealing the strange marks at the bottom to be—

"Numbers! Captain, aren't they—?"

"Longitude and latitude coordinates!"

"Do you know the location?"

Haddock slowly lowered the parchment. "I do."

"Well, what are we waiting for?" Tintin cried. "Let's go!"

CHAPTER TEN

★

Home Again

"**Marlinspike Hall!** The coordinates lead to your family home?"

When Haddock told him where they were headed, Tintin couldn't believe it. But the captain was certain that was where the scrolls led.

And now they were inside the tall iron gates. Once a well-maintained sprawling estate, with a stately mansion and well-kept gardens, Marlinspike Hall had lately fallen into disrepair. Still, as they walked to the front door, Captain Haddock smiled at the crumbling walls with affection.

"I don't think it's changed since I was a boy." He withdrew an old, rusty key from his pocket. But before he could insert it into the lock, the door opened.

"Hello, sir, and welcome back to Marlinspike Hall," a prim butler said.

Haddock's jaw dropped. "Nestor! You're still here? But—but it's been *years* since any of my family has lived here!"

Nestor tilted his head. "Your grandfather made arrangements for me to remain at Marlinspike Hall after his death. He believed that one day a Haddock would return to take charge of the estate. It seems he was correct."

Haddock sighed heavily. "There's no way I could afford to live here."

Tintin held up the scrolls. "Don't give up yet!" He surveyed the hallway. "Where to?"

"Let's try the cellar," the captain said.

They hurried down stone steps into a dank underground room. Haddock looked puzzled. "I meant the other cellar."

"There is no other cellar, sir," Nestor said.

Just then, Snowy gave a muffled bark.

"Snowy, where are you?" Tintin called.

Snowy barked again.

"He's behind that pile of old furniture!"

They shifted the pile piece by piece. Behind it was a brick wall.

"Look! A hole!" Haddock exclaimed. He put his eye to the opening.

"What do you see?" Tintin asked eagerly.

"Your dog," he said. "A roomful of old furnishings. And…"

"And?" Tintin prodded.

"And something that doesn't exist."

Together, they removed bricks to enlarge the opening. Then they crawled through, and Haddock led Tintin over to a beautiful globe of Earth. Haddock looked at it for a minute, pondering. "This island," he suddenly said, pointing to a tiny raised dot on the globe, "doesn't exist."

"How do you know?" Tintin asked.

"I'm a Haddock. The sea is in my blood. This

island is a mistake!" He jabbed his finger at the dot.

Suddenly, the globe sprang open. And there, winking at them from its longtime resting place, was an old sea captain's hat filled with glittering jewels!

"The treasure!" Tintin and Haddock yelled together.

Haddock removed a diamond necklace with gentle fingers. "To think, it's been here all these years."

"Yes," Tintin agreed. "And there's something else here, too." He reached into the globe and pulled out an ancient piece of parchment.

"Not another scroll!" Haddock groaned.

Tintin unrolled it carefully. "It's a map. Unless I'm wrong, it leads to a four-hundred-year-old wreck."

Haddock's eyes widened. "The *Unicorn*?"

Tintin grinned. "And all the treasure that sank with her. So how's your thirst for adventure, Captain?"

"Unquenchable!"

"Then what are we waiting for?" Tintin whistled for Snowy. "Let's go!"